IVASIONS & CONQUESTS

SLAMIC PERIOD
38-1099 C.E.

CRUSADER PERIOD
1099-1260 C.E.

LATE ISLAMIC PERIOD
1260-1516 C.E.

OTTOMAN PERIOD
1516-1917

BRITISH RULE
1917-1948

ISRAELI RULE
1948-PRESENT

Jerusalem 3000

Kids Discover the City of Gold!

Jerusalem 3000

Kids Discover the City of Gold!

Design: Benjie Herskowitz

Published by PITSPOPANY PRESS

ISBN: 0-943706-59-9

Printed in Jerusalem, Israel

Jerusalem 3000
Kids Discover the City of Gold!

by Alan Paris
Illustrated by PeterG

PITSPOPANY

NEW YORK ◊ JERUSALEM

TABLE OF CONTENTS

INTRODUCTION

Kids!
Discover the City of Gold!

Jerusalem is known by many names, including the City of Gold, the City of Beauty, the City of God, and the City of David.

Enter Jerusalem and you enter the portals of a city where time takes on new meaning.

The ancient houses and modern shops are crowded with people wearing robes and sandals and others wearing suits and ties. It's like a mixture of centuries crammed into a small, beautiful corner of the world.

Jerusalem.

To understand the beauty of Jerusalem, just turn these pages. The story before each illustration tells you about the scenes that are portrayed.

Tamar and Shalom, our two bubble travelers, are your guides through Jerusalem. Like many of you, this is Shalom's first trip to Jerusalem. Tamar, on the other hand, has been

TAMAR

SHALOM

here before, and helps him — and you — understand what these spectacular sites represent.

After you read about each site, turn to the illustration. The picture on the left reveals how the scene appeared long ago. The picture on the right shows you how it looks today. There are many fascinating details in the pictures. Sometimes Tamar and Shalom point them out, and sometimes, if you look closely, you'll find them yourself.

There are even "Did You Know?" bubbles which give you some facts that most people, even Israelis, might not know.

Jerusalem 3000: Kids Discover the City of Gold! was originally created to help kids celebrate the 3000th birthday of Jerusalem. But it is also your chance to discover the one place in the world where time takes on new meaning; where the past, present, and future unite to create a city which is the home of the Jewish people.

Jerusalem.

CITY OF DAVID

 1004 B.C.E. **K**ing David conquered the city of Jebus from the Jebusites, a mixture of the Amorite and Hittite peoples from the area of present-day Syria and Turkey in the year 1004 B.C.E.

When the Israelites made Jebus their capital, they changed its name to Jerusalem, which also became known as the City of David. The city was located on the slope above the main source of water, the Gihon Spring.

King David had many good reasons for wanting Jerusalem to be the new capital of the Israelite nation. Jerusalem was centrally located in the midst of all 12 tribes of Israel. It was also far from any borders, which made it easier to defend against attack.

King David knew that Jerusalem would not be complete without the Ark of the Covenant, which was the symbol of unity for the Israelites. Up to this time, the Ark, which housed the Ten Commandments, did not have a permanent home. It was kept in the Tabernacle, which was built by the Israelites after their exodus from Egypt. They carried it with them during their 40 years of wandering through the desert. When they entered the Land of Israel, they began planning a permanent home for the Tabernacle.

Two years after King David conquered the city, he brought the Ark to Jerusalem. King David planned to build a permanent building to house the Ark, which became known as the First Temple. Unfortunately, through most of his reign, King David was kept busy fighting the nations around him and strengthening the military power of his kingdom. He had many enemies, especially the Philistines who lived on the plains near

DID YOU KNOW?

In the Bible, Mount Moriah was the place on which Abraham was commanded to sacrifice his son, Isaac. It was also where Jacob had his dream about the ladder with angels ascending to and descending from heaven. Of course, this is also the site where King Solomon built the First Temple, the place of worship for the Israelite nation.

SHALOM: *So this is Jerusalem! I never saw so many different types of buildings. There are skyscrapers next to red-roofed houses. That building in front of us looks like a small Empire State Building and the other one to the right looks very royal. What are those buildings?*

TAMAR: *The one in front is the King Solomon Hotel and that one over there is the famous King David Hotel. Sort of a father-and-son combination.*

SHALOM: *What's so famous about the King David Hotel?*

TAMAR: *Well, for one thing, every diplomat who ever came to Israel has stayed in that hotel. For another, part of it was blown up in 1946 by a Jewish underground movement, as a protest against British rule here.*

SHALOM: *Look! There's a wedding procession down there! They must be famous. Look at all the photographers.*

TAMAR: *That's not a wedding procession, Shalom. Brides and grooms always come to be photographed in the Yemin Moshe Park. It's a kind of tradition.*

SHALOM: *What else is going on in the city?*

TAMAR: *That's what we're about to find out. So, hold onto your bubble. Welcome to Jerusalem, the City of David, where 3,000 years of Jewish history is just waiting to be discovered.*

● ●

the Mediterranean Sea. It would fall upon his son, the famous King Solomon, to build the First Temple.

After the conquest of Jerusalem, King David purchased the Threshing Floor of Araunah on Mount Moriah. Araunah was probably the last ruler of Jebus before King David conquered it. On this spot the Temple would be built.

The Bible tells us that King David was a man of war and that his hands were covered with the blood of his enemies. That is why he did not have the privilege of building the Temple, which was to be a place of peace.

When King David died in 970 B.C.E., Solomon, who was just 16 years old, took the throne. Thanks to the good job that his father had done in crushing Israel's enemies, Solomon's 40-year reign was peaceful and prosperous. This provided him with the time and money needed to build the First Temple and beautify the city of Jerusalem.

King Solomon began construction of the Temple four years after the death of his father and completed it in seven years.

King David's Jerusalem had a wall around it and at the northern tip of the city was his palace. The whole city was pretty small, with a population of probably not more than several thousand people. Today, Jerusalem, the largest city in Israel, has a population of over 500,000.

● ●

KING DAVID

King David is primarily known as the second Hebrew King. However, he also had considerable musical skill. He played the harp and wrote poetry throughout his life. The Book of Psalms contains many of King David's writings.

● ● ● ● ● ● ● ● ● ● ● ● ● ● ● ● ● ● ●

DID YOU KNOW?

In 1867, Charles Warren, an English explorer, discovered a shaft carved in rock which descends from the City of David to the Gihon Spring. Perhaps King David used this water shaft to secretly enter the city and capture it from the Jebusites.

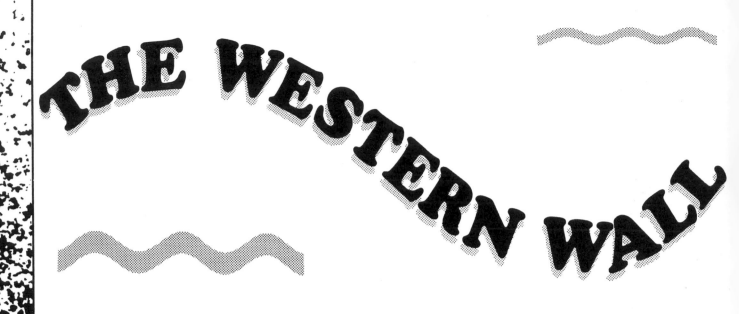

THE WESTERN WALL

Most of the Western Wall that is visible today is more than 2,000 years old. It was built as one of the walls supporting the raised area upon which the Second Temple stood.

In those days, as today, a second wall surrounded the entire city of Jerusalem. This outside wall was built to protect the people living there from their enemies. The only way in or out was through one of the many gates in the wall.

Today, the Western Wall, or the *Kotel*, which means "wall" in Hebrew, is inside what is called the Old City. Until about 150 years ago, the Old City comprised all of Jerusalem. The walls of the Old City are still visible today.

959 B.C.E. The First Temple was originally constructed by King Solomon on Mount Moriah in 959 B.C.E. Tragically, it was destroyed in 586 B.C.E. by the Babylonians, who sent the surviving Jews of Jerusalem into exile in Babylon.

516 B.C.E. After 70 years in exile, the Second Temple was built. The Persian King, Cyrus the Great, who conquered the Babylonians, gave the Jews the opportunity to return to Jerusalem and allowed them to rebuild their Temple.

Persian control lasted until Alexander the Great conquered Jerusalem in 332 B.C.E. The Temple was not harmed by Alexander.

In 167 B.C.E., Jerusalem was ruled by Antiochus Epiphanes, King of the Seleucid Empire. He angered the Jews when he set up Greek gods in the Temple.

SHALOM: *Jerusalem is celebrating its 3,000th birthday, and I hear they're going to have the world's biggest birthday cake. There sure seems to be plenty to celebrate about.*

TAMAR: *I'll say! There may be a capital older than Jerusalem, but I'll bet there's none with more history. Look at the people down there, praying and dancing at the Western Wall.*

SHALOM: *Hey, isn't that a Bar Mitzvah boy in front of the Wall, reading from the Torah? And look, over there a man is putting a little piece of paper into a crack in the Wall. That's strange!*

TAMAR: *It's part of Jewish tradition, Shalom. This is close to the place where the Temple stood. People write their prayers on a piece of paper and put them into the Wall, hoping their prayers will go right up to the throne of God.*

SHALOM: *It's hard to believe that one wall, no matter how old, can have such an effect on people.*

TAMAR: *That's because the Western Wall is the heart of the Jewish people, just like Jerusalem is the heart of Israel.*

●●●

164 B.C.E. The Hasmonean Priests, who were also known as the Maccabees, went to war against Antiochus to regain control of Jerusalem and the Temple. They defeated his mighty army in 164 B.C.E. It is this victory that Jews commemorate by celebrating the Festival of Hanukkah.

37 B.C.E. In 63 B.C.E., the Roman Empire wrested control of Jerusalem from the Hasmonean rulers and in 37 B.C.E. installed Herod as the new king of Israel. King Herod remodeled the Temple and made it into an awe-inspiring structure.

In order to enlarge the area of the Temple, Herod built huge supporting walls to help secure the foundation where the Temple stood. It is the remains of one of these walls that is known today as the Western Wall.

70 C.E. The Jews were not happy living under the yoke of Rome and rebelled in 70 C.E., but their fight for freedom failed. After a long siege, the Romans destroyed the Temple, along with most of the city. Once again, the survivors of the destruction of Jerusalem were exiled, this time to Rome and other parts of the Roman Empire.

1948 For 2,000 years, following the destruction of the Second Temple, the exiled Jews wandered throughout the world. They never stopped praying to return to Israel. Finally, their prayers were answered when, in 1948, the modern State of Israel was proclaimed as the Homeland of the Jewish People. Since then, the Jewish People have been returning to their Promised Land.

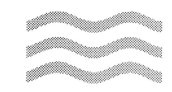

DID YOU KNOW?

Tisha B'Av

According to Jewish tradition, both the First and Second Temples were destroyed on the 9th day of the Hebrew month of Av (Tisha B'Av) more than 650 years apart.

Because of this double tragedy, Tisha B'Av, in the Jewish calendar is a day of fasting, a time to mourn the destruction of the holiest Jewish site.

Tens of thousands of people stream into Jerusalem on this day to pray at the Western Wall.

THE CARDO

Nearly all Roman and Byzantine cities were planned with two main streets, one running north-south called a *Cardo* and the other, running east-west, called a *Decumanus*.

The Cardo was paved with very large stones, worn smooth by the many carts and animals which passed over it. Raised a bit above the street were sidewalks for pedestrians. A row of high stone columns running the entire length of the street on both sides separated the traffic from the pedestrians. The areas between the columns and the shops were roofed so that people could walk and do their shopping protected from the hot sun in the summer and the rain and wind in the winter, very much like the shopping malls of today!

70 C.E. After the Romans conquered Jerusalem and destroyed the Second Temple in 70 C.E., they leveled what remained of the city's palaces, mansions and public buildings. Jerusalem was an example of what would happen to any nation which dared to rebel against the mighty Roman Empire.

132 C.E. The Roman Legions were stationed in bases built over the ruins of Jerusalem. The name of the city was eventually changed to Aelia Capitolina which combines the name of the Roman Emperor Publius Aelius Hadrian (ruled from 117-138 C.E.) with that of Jupiter Capitolinus, a god of the Romans.

The Roman Emperor Hadrian was virulently anti-Jewish. He enacted a series of laws which

DID YOU KNOW?

Ancient Coins

Ancient coins can tell us interesting things about the history of Jerusalem. Bar-Kochba issued coins during his rebellion against the Romans. Many of these show pictures of musical instruments and other objects used in the Temple.

Some of these say "For the freedom of Jerusalem." After the Romans crushed the Jewish rebellion in 70 C.E. and destroyed the city, they issued special coins to commemorate the event.

Some of these coins show the symbol of conquered Judea.

The words Iudaea Capta mean "Judea conquered."

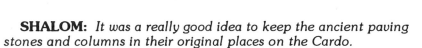

SHALOM: *It was a really good idea to keep the ancient paving stones and columns in their original places on the Cardo.*

TAMAR: *It's like walking down an old Roman street. You feel that a chariot will come whizzing by any second.*

SHALOM: *Well, if it does we can always duck into one of those modern art galleries or souvenir shops. And there's a restaurant where you can put on a toga and eat and drink Roman food out of clay bowls and cups, just like in Roman times. I'm hungry, Tamar. Let's go there.*

●●

prohibited Jews from practicing their religion, and made Jewish education punishable by death.

But it was Hadrian's decision, in 132 C.E., to build a temple to Jupiter on the ruins of the Jewish Temple that finally provoked a massive rebellion among the people, led by Shimon Bar-Kochba. The famous Rabbi Akiva was the spiritual leader of the rebellion and he saw in Bar-Kochba a leader who could bring about the Messianic Era.

Within a few short years, however, the Romans succeeded in crushing the rebellion and with it the hope of an independent Jewish country.

The Romans then went ahead with their plans to turn Jerusalem into a truly Roman city. They built temples to their gods and did not allow Jews to live in Jerusalem.

 The pagan Romans controlled the city until 324 C.E., when the Roman Emperor Constantine adopted Christianity as the official religion of his empire. Constantine's rule marks the beginning of what is today called the Byzantine period of history.

During this period, Jerusalem became the most important religious center in the Byzantine Christian Empire. The official name of the city became Aelia, with the pagan "Capitolina" removed. The Byzantine period lasted until the year 638 C.E.

The Romans built a Cardo in Jerusalem as they did in all the major cities under their rule. It became the main street of Jerusalem. People shopped at the Cardo for both local goods and merchandise imported from other parts of the world. The Cardo started at what is today the Damascus Gate, one of the entrances to the walled Old City. Beneath the present-day Damascus Gate, archaeologists have uncovered the entrance to the city during the Roman-Byzantine period and the plaza where the Cardo began.

SULTAN'S POOL

During the Second Temple period, providing water to the people in Jerusalem was a constant problem, especially during the three major Jewish holidays of Passover, Shavuot, and Sukkot. At these times, tens of thousands of Jews would converge on the city to pray at the Temple, and vast quantities of water were needed.

Water was brought to Jerusalem in pipelines and aqueducts over long distances. The water was stored in pools which were carved into the bedrock in different parts of the city. One such pool, known as the Snakes Pool, was located in the Valley of Hinnom. The Ottoman Sultan, Suleiman the Magnificent (1496-1566), who built the walls around the Old City of Jerusalem that we still see today, repaired and enlarged the Snakes Pool. It has been called the Sultan's Pool ever since.

950 B.C.E. But the Valley was known for more than just water. The prophets of the Bible describe the Valley of Hinnom, *Ge-Hinnom* in Hebrew, as a hotbed of idol worship. In the Valley, people built pagan altars in a place called the *Tophet,* which means "place of fire." The Tophet was located at the foot of Mount Zion. There, pagan worshippers lit fires, burned incense and offered sacrifices. Some even offered their own children as sacrifices to *Moloch,* an Ammonite idol.

620 B.C.E. Fortunately, King Josiah of Judah put an end to these horrible practices by destroying these altars around 620 B.C.E. The word, *Gehinnom*, has come to mean "Hell" in the Hebrew language.

TAMAR: *I never thought we would be visiting Ge-Hinnom during our trip to Jerusalem, but here we are!*

SHALOM: *I can't believe people actually sacrificed to idols down there. It's so green and peaceful. And the view of the walls of the Old City and Mount Zion is really spectacular.*

TAMAR: *I hear the acoustics at the Sultan's Pool are pretty spectacular as well.*

SHALOM: *I can't wait to go swimming. When do they turn on the water?*

TAMAR: *Actually, there hasn't been any water there for a long time.*

SHALOM: *Then why is there a sign down there saying "Major Waves" due in today?*

TAMAR: *That's a rock group. They're performing tonight. And we've got front row seats!*

●●

1800 By the last century, the Sultan's Pool was no longer used as a storage reservoir. It had fallen into disrepair. It eventually became the site of a cattle market because there was plenty of water for the cows to drink.

1948 When the Jewish Quarter in Jerusalem fell to the Arab Legion in 1948, Israeli soldiers were trapped on Mount Zion. Arab soldiers stood on the Old City walls shooting at anyone trying to bring supplies in. They wouldn't even allow the wounded to be evacuated. So, the Israelis came up with a brilliant idea! They decided to string a cable across the Valley of Hinnom, from Mount Zion on one side to the Eye Hospital on the other. At night, a trolley was hung from the cable and pulled back and forth to provide food, water, medicine and other supplies for the Jewish soldiers on Mount Zion.

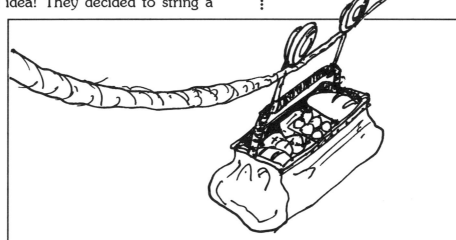

Sometimes people were transported back and forth. This cable may still be seen today, though the trolley is no longer used.

Today, the Sultan's Pool has been turned into a giant, open-air concert hall, where people gather to hear everything from rock music to symphony orchestras. Nearby is the Jerusalem Cinematheque, which has a huge film library and shows old and new movies.

JAFFA GATE

1516 The Moslem Ottoman Turks gained control over Jerusalem in 1516. The Ottomans permitted and even encouraged Jewish refugees expelled from Spain and Portugal to settle in their empire. The Ottoman rulers knew that an active Jewish community would help to develop and expand their economy.

Just as King Solomon had built Jerusalem into a great city some 2,500 years earlier, the Ottoman Sultan Suleiman (Solomon in Arabic!), nicknamed "the Magnificent," rebuilt Jerusalem, beginning in 1542. It was under Ottoman rule that the Western Wall became a place of prayer for the Jews.

Many of the most beautiful sites in Jerusalem today were built or restored when the Ottomans controlled the city from 1516-1917. These include the walls around the Old City, and the seven gates in these walls.

One of the most important gates to Jerusalem was, and remains, the Jaffa Gate. From this gate, a road leads westward to Jaffa, the port city on the Mediterranean Coast which today forms part of the city of Tel Aviv. Jaffa was once Jerusalem's main connection with the rest of the world. Boats arriving at Jaffa brought religious Jewish, Christian and Moslem pilgrims to Jerusalem. Products from distant lands were transported up the steep road

DID YOU KNOW?

Tradition says that Sinan, the architect for Suleiman the Magnificent, was put to death by the sultan after he rebuilt the walls of the Old City of Jerusalem. The reason given is that Sinan forgot to include Mount Zion within the walls. This hill is so important in the tradition of the city that Jerusalem is frequently called "Zion" in the Bible.

SHALOM: *Here's a giant doorway in the stone wall around the Old City. Let's go inside.*

TAMAR: *This is the Jaffa Gate, one of the main entrances to the Old City of Jerusalem.*

SHALOM: *I don't think I've ever seen people dressed in so many different ways and wearing so many different kinds of hats!*

TAMAR: *That Hasid is wearing a shtreimel, a hat made out of fur. The Armenian Bishop is wearing a pointed hat shaped like the peak of Mount Ararat in Armenia. And that Arab villager is wearing a keffiye, a scarf with a black band called an* aqal *to hold it in place.*

SHALOM: *What about the man with the bread-hat on his head?*

TAMAR: *That isn't a hat! That's how the bakers carry trays of fresh bread to their shops!*

●●

to Jerusalem and entered the city through the Jaffa Gate.

 The area just outside this gate and the square which opens from it, were among the busiest places in Jerusalem a century ago. Many hotels were built where visitors to the city could stay. There was regular stagecoach service for passengers travelling between Jerusalem and Jaffa. Many European countries established banks, post offices and even consulates in Jerusalem.

Ottoman control over Jerusalem lasted until 1917, when the Ottoman Army was defeated by the British in World War I.

Today, the Jaffa Gate has been enlarged to accommodate cars filled with tourists who visit the Arab *shuk or* market, David's Tower, or to wind their way through the Old City to the Western Wall.

DID YOU KNOW?

Today, everyone has a wristwatch and there are clocks in all houses and public buildings. But during the Ottoman rule in Jerusalem, only very wealthy people had their own clocks and watches. In 1907, a clock tower was built inside the Jaffa Gate. This tower had dials indicating both European and Arabic hours. It was removed by the British soon after they conquered the city since it was a symbol of Ottoman control over the city.

THE CITADEL

The Jerusalem Citadel is located next to Jaffa Gate, which is the main gate into the Old City. The Citadel was first constructed during the period of the Hasmoneans around 150 B.C.E. This was the best location for a military observation post because it provided soldiers with a superb view of the main roads leading into the city from the west.

High watchtowers were built onto the Citadel in order to provide an even better view. No opposing armies could mount a sneak attack against the city as long as soldiers manned the ramparts of the Citadel. If an army did manage to penetrate the city's outer defenses, they would still find it very difficult to storm the Citadel. A wide, deep moat, filled with water ran around the Citadel. With the archers above, it was almost impossible to get across this moat. Today, while the moat is still visible, there is no water in it.

37 B.C.E. During King Herod's reign (37-4 B.C.E), he built three watchtowers, not only for defense, but also to glorify the memories of Hippicus, his friend, Phasael, his brother, and Mariamne, his wife. These huge towers dominated the skyline of Herodian Jerusalem and were made of white marble, precisely cut into blocks 30 feet long, 15 feet wide and 7.5 feet deep. These blocks were joined, one to the other, so perfectly that each tower looked like a single polished rock reaching towards the sky.

Inside the Phasael Tower were magnificent apartments and even a swimming pool. Historians

DID YOU KNOW?

Today, inside the large courtyard of the Citadel, you can see a special sound and light show which traces Jerusalem's 3,000 year history. The Citadel Museum presents exhibits showing what people ate, how they dressed, and what kind of work they did during different periods of the city's history.

TAMAR: *Keep your head down, Shalom, we're flying through the Jaffa Gate. Do you know what that building is with the moat around it?*

SHALOM: *Camelot?*

TAMAR: *Very funny! That's the Citadel. But I suppose in one sense you're right. The Citadel, like the castles in England, was meant to be a fortress that could protect the city. Actually the words citadel and fortress mean the same thing today. In ancient times, soldiers were stationed around the ramparts of the Citadel to keep an eye out for the enemy.*

SHALOM: *And that tall tower over there must be where they sent traitors and enemy knights who were waiting to be beheaded by the guillotine.*

TAMAR: *They never used the guillotine in Jerusalem. That's a watchtower. One of the rulers of Jerusalem built it in memory of someone dear to him. Today, it's called the Tower of David. Come on, let's go inside.*

● ●

calculate that the Phasael Tower was 135 feet high, making it one of the tallest buildings of ancient times. It probably seemed much taller to those who saw it, because it was built on a high hill.

The Hippicus Tower had a 30-foot deep reservoir for rainwater and a two-story palace in its upper portion.

The Mariamne Tower was the smallest of the three towers, standing only 82 feet high, but was the most elaborate.

70 C.E. Although Titus, the Roman conqueror, destroyed the Second Temple and Jerusalem in 70 C.E., he left Herod's three towers standing. The Citadel continued to be used to protect Jerusalem during the Roman, Byzantine and following periods.

After the Moslem conquest of Jerusalem in 638 C.E., new walls and towers were built to protect the city from outsiders. These remained until the Christians conquered Jerusalem in 1099 C.E. The Citadel was then significantly enlarged to protect the city against renewed Moslem attacks.

It was the Crusaders who actually gave one of Herod's three towers its present name, The Tower of David. Since it was one of the largest structures in Jerusalem, the Christians associated the tower with King David, even though it did not exist during David's reign.

Actually, historians are not sure which of Herod's three towers is today's Tower of David. The massive structure we see today is really just the base of Herod's original tower. It is a 66-foot square, standing 66 feet high, probably less than half its original height.

DID YOU KNOW?

Archaeologists have found ancient ammunition outside of the Citadel. Large *ballista stones,* stone balls about the size of bowling balls, and smaller *sling stones,* about the size of marbles, were hurled at the Citadel by the invading armies.

29

THE JEWISH QUARTER

DID YOU KNOW?

In 1870, Emperor Franz Joseph of Austria visited Jerusalem and was taken to visit the Jewish Quarter of the Old City. The Tiferet Israel Synagogue had not been completed for lack of funds. When the emperor asked about the unfinished dome of the building, he was told:

"As a man removes his hat to greet a distinguished visitor, the dome of the building has been removed to greet you!"

The emperor then donated the money necessary to complete the domed roof of Tiferet Israel.

1516 The Jewish Quarter is one of the four quarters, or neighborhoods, in the Old City. The other neighborhoods are the Moslem, Christian and Armenian quarters.
While different neighborhoods existed before the Ottoman Turks took control of Jerusalem in 1516, it was during their rule that the four quarters became firmly established. The Jewish community prospered during Ottoman rule and its population increased.

1701 In 1701, Rabbi Yehuda Hasid arrived in Jerusalem from Europe with a group of his followers. They began to build a synagogue in the Jewish Quarter, but after a short time Rabbi Yehuda died. In 1720, the unfinished synagogue was torched and his followers were forced to leave Jerusalem by the ruling authorities.
What remained of the synagogue was called the *Hurva*, which means "ruin" in Hebrew. It was all that was left of Rabbi Yehuda's dream.

1857 About 150 years after Rabbi Yehuda started to build his synagogue, the Jewish community was able to raise the necessary funds to finish the project. Finally, in 1857, the largest synagogue in the Jewish Quarter of the Old City of Jerusalem was built. It towered majestically over the small stone houses, its high, domed roof visible above all the other buildings. This synagogue continued to serve the Jewish community until Israel's independence in 1948.

1948 When Israel proclaimed itself a Jewish state, it was immediately attacked by the Arab armies. The Arab Legion (the army of the Kingdom of Jordan) occupied the Old City of Jerusalem and held the remaining Jews hostage until a cease-fire was called.

SHALOM: *Hang on to your bubble, Tamar. There's something very strange going on. The wind is blowing that old man's books straight up to the sky.*

TAMAR: *I've got one of the books, Shalom. Let's see what it says.*

SHALOM: *It's a siddur, a prayer book. Look how old it is.*

TAMAR: *It must have come from the Hurva Synagogue in the Old City.*

SHALOM: *But the Hurva was destroyed almost 50 years ago.*

TAMAR: *The synagogue was destroyed, but the prayers that were recited in the Hurva go on forever.*

• •

After the Jordanians took control of the eastern half of Jerusalem, no Jew was allowed to live in that part of the city, which included the Jewish Quarter of the Old City.

Jews were not even allowed to visit the Western Wall, or bury their dead in the ancient Jewish cemetery on the Mount of Olives. They could only cherish their memories of these places and hope that, someday, it would again be possible to visit them.

The Arab Legion systematically destroyed the synagogues, hospitals and homes in the Jewish Quarter. This was their way of ensuring that the Jews would have nothing to return to in the Old City. Once again, the Hurva was destroyed and left in ruins.

1967 When Israel miraculously won the Six-Day War in June 1967, the Arab Legion was forced out of Jerusalem and Jews triumphantly returned to the Jewish Quarter of the Old City.

Unfortunately, the Hurva Synagogue had been destroyed beyond repair and the decision was made not to rebuild it. Instead, a single archway of the building was reconstructed as a memorial.

Other synagogues in the Jewish Quarter were restored to their former beauty. And today, once again, these synagogues and the Western Wall are places of prayer for Jewish residents and visitors to the city.

The homes, courtyards and shops of the Jewish Quarter, all destroyed by the Arab Legion, have also been beautifully rebuilt. Today a vibrant community flourishes in the heart of Jerusalem's Old City.

DID YOU KNOW?

The Temple Institute, located in the middle of the Jewish Quarter, has recreated many of the utensils used in the Temple, as well as the garments worn by the Priests. The golden seven-branch *Menorah* and incense used for the sacrifices are among dozens of objects on display.

YEMIN MOSHE

(1800) During the 1800s, the Jewish Quarter of the Old City, where most of the Jews lived, was the smallest of the city's four quarters in actual size, but held the most people.

As the population grew, families lived in tiny apartments, sometimes with as many as six or more people in a room. Besides overcrowding, there wasn't enough water or a proper sewage system.

(1860) The Ottoman Turks ruled during this period. They kept Jerusalem and the countryside around it safe from marauders. So, for the first time in a long while, it became possible to consider building outside the city walls.

Sir Moses Montefiore (1784-1885), was an English Jew who gave generously to the Jewish community of Jerusalem. After visiting the Old City and witnessing the difficult conditions under which the residents lived, Montefiore arranged for the design and development of the first neighborhood to be built outside the Old City walls, *Mishkenot Sha'ananim*, or "Calm Dwellings" in English. The funding for this project came from the trust fund of Judah Toura (1776-1854), an American Jew from New Orleans.

Sir Moses also built a windmill in the area to help the residents support themselves. They ground wheat not only to make their own bread, but to sell within the Old City as well.

Initially, people were afraid to leave the familiar surroundings and security of the Old City. In fact, at night after work, many people returned to the safety of the walls. It took a while, but as people got used to this new type of neighborhood, they gradually began

DID YOU KNOW?

Stones With Heart

When Sir Moses Montefiore met with the Turkish Sultan he was asked why the stones of the Western Wall were so important to the Jews. Montefiore answered, "You must understand, Your Majesty, there are people with hearts of stone, and stones with the hearts of people."

SHALOM: *Oops! We made a wrong turn somewhere! There's a windmill down there!*

TAMAR: *That's the Yemin Moshe windmill. It's a museum today, although people used it a hundred years ago.*

SHALOM: *What about that Cinderella carriage at the bottom of the windmill? Don't tell me it carried a princess a hundred years ago.*

TAMAR: *No, it didn't carry a princess. That's the carriage of Sir Moses Montefiore, and for the Jews in Israel he was more like a prince, helping everyone he could. He's a hero and a legend in Jerusalem.*

SHALOM: *Hey! Aren't those tulips down there? Are you sure this is Jerusalem?*

TAMAR: *Sure it is! If you don't believe me, let's visit Yemin Moshe and you'll see for yourself.*

living and working permanently outside of the Old City walls.

Mishkenot Sha'ananim eventually became part of a larger neighborhood, called *Yemin Moshe*, "The Right Hand of Moses" in English, in honor of Sir Moses Montefiore.

During Israel's War of Independence, the Arab Legion occupied the Old City, and the neighborhood of Yemin Moshe became the front line in the battle between Arabs and Jews. The windmill, because of its height, was an excellent observation post from which Israeli soldiers could monitor the Arab Legion's activities.

Shots were fired back and forth across the Valley of Hinnom, which separates Yemin Moshe from the Old City. It became quite dangerous and while many residents abandoned Yemin Moshe, a faithful few remained and fought. By the end of the War of Independence, many of the homes in the neighborhood had been severely damaged. Even after the cease-fire, Arab snipers continued firing from the walls of the Old City into Yemin Moshe. Tragically, Montefiore's dream community was no longer a safe place to live.

After Israel's victory in the Six-Day War, Jerusalem was reunified under Israeli rule. Yemin Moshe underwent a renovation program that transformed it into one of the most beautiful neighborhoods in the city. Today, many artists and writers live there.

Mishkenot Sha'ananim, Montefiore's original neighborhood within Yemin Moshe, has become a center for the arts. Famous painters, sculptors and artisans from around the world are invited to take up residence for a set period of time, while they create a work of art inspired by the city of Jerusalem.

DID YOU KNOW?

Many neighborhoods in modern Jerusalem bear Sir Moses Montefiore's Hebrew name, Moshe. These places include Ohel Moshe, Mazkeret Moshe, Yemin Moshe and Kiryat Moshe.

JERUSALEM 4000

What do you imagine Jerusalem will be like in 1,000 years?

What if you could stand in your room, touch a virtual reality screen and presto! the Western Wall pops up in front of you.

You could invite all your friends to celebrate your Bar or Bat Mitzvah at the Wall, without leaving your living room.

Want to speak to King David? No problem. Point your wand and winko! King David stands in front of you, ready to discuss his latest battle or help you with a problem of your own.

Enemies? There won't be any. Israel will live in peace. Anti-semitism...racial hatred...jealousy...poverty...all gone! People will respect each other's beliefs and opinions. Best of all, Israel *will* be a light unto the nations.

A dream?

Perhaps. But think. When most of you were born no

SHALOM: *This is your captain speaking. We've arrived in Jerusalem, the capital of Israel. You can unfasten your seat belts now. I've made another perfect landing.*

TAMAR: *Stop it Shalom! We've been on automatic pilot right from the start. You never even touched the controls.*

SHALOM: *Well, I saw a film of the olden days and that's what they used to say.*

TAMAR: *But these are the Golden Days, Shalom. People don't worry about seatbelts or crashing. You can fax yourself or fly like we did. And besides, Jerusalem is no longer just the capital of Israel, it's the capital of the world, of all the worlds in our solar system.*

SHALOM: *Who doesn't know that! Anyway, we've landed. Let's go to the Temple. I hear they're choosing a new High Priest today.*

TAMAR: *O.K. But after that I want you to take a picture of me with the lion and the lamb.*

SHALOM: *It's hard to believe that lions actually ate lambs.*

TAMAR: *That was part of the olden days too, Shalom. Now aren't you glad those times are over?*

SHALOM: *I guess so. Especially since kids my age actually had to leave their homes to go to a place called school.*

TAMAR: *I'm sure glad there aren't any of those places around anymore. Come on, we don't want to miss the Temple Express.*

◆◆◆◆◆◆◆◆◆◆◆◆◆◆◆◆◆◆◆◆◆◆◆◆◆◆ ◆◆◆◆◆◆◆◆◆◆◆◆◆◆◆◆◆◆◆◆◆◆◆◆◆◆

one had ever heard of a fax or a compact disc or virtual reality. The world changes drastically about every 20 years. Creating lakes in the Judean desert and hot springs on the top of Mount Hermon are almost within our reach. In a thousand years it will be child's play...literally!

You don't believe it? Wait and see.

INVASIONS & CONQUESTS

Jerusalem today is a lively, modern city shaped by its past. The city's three thousand year history includes numerous invasions, conquests, destructions and rebuildings.

On these pages, the history of the invasions and conquests of Jerusalem has been divided into different time periods, beginning with the Jebusite period and proceeding, in order, up to the modern State of Israel.

To see how these conquerers looked, turn to the time line on the inside of the cover.

Jebusite Period
1300-1004 B.C.E.

What little we know about the Jebusites comes from biblical descriptions of how King David conquered the city of Jebus from them. They were a mixture of Amorites and Hittites, two ancient peoples from the area of present-day Syria and Turkey.

The Jebusites had lived in Jebus, their capital, for generations when King David arrived with the Israelite army. His clever strategy for conquering the heavily fortified city probably involved routing his troops through the tunnel that brought water into the city from the Gihon Spring. After King David conquered Jebus, he allowed many Jebusites to remain living in the city alongside the Israelites.

King David
1004-970 B.C.E.

After he conquered Jebus, King David began developing the city, making it the capital of his kingdom. By bringing the Ark of the Covenant to Jerusalem, he also made the city into the spiritual center of the 12 Israelite tribes.

During his reign, King David was kept busy defending his kingdom against the neighboring Philistines, Ammonites, Moabites and Aramaeans. In addition, he expanded the kingdom's territory to make it stronger and more secure.

When King David died in 970 B.C.E., his son, Solomon, took over the throne and continued to build and expand the city of Jerusalem. Because his father had worked so hard to secure the kingdom's territory, King Solomon was able to devote his efforts primarily to developing the city and improving governmental administration.

King Solomon built the First Temple which King David had envisioned. Under his rule, Jerusalem became a magnificent city, known world-wide for its beauty and prosperity.

When King Solomon died, the kingdom split into two parts. The Northern Kingdom, called Israel, had

its capital at Samaria and was destroyed by Assyrian invaders in 722 B.C.E. The Southern Kingdom, called Judah, with Jerusalem as its capital, survived until 586 B.C.E.

Babylonian Conquest
586 B.C.E.

It was very difficult for the tiny Kingdom of Judah to remain independent because of the pressures imposed upon it by neighboring Egypt and Assyria. There were repeated invasions by these superpowers.

In 586 B.C.E., Jerusalem was invaded by the Babylonians, successors to the Assyrians. The city's fortifications and Temple were destroyed. The leading Judean families were deported to Babylon in what has become known as the Babylonian Exile.

Though far from their homeland, the Jews continued to practice their religion and did not forget Jerusalem. Their longing to return was finally satisfied after the Persians overthrew the Babylonians.

The new rulers allowed the Jews to return to Jerusalem. The small community grew under Persian control and in 516 B.C.E., seventy years after being exiled, the Jewish community was able to rebuild the Temple.

Alexander the Great
332 B.C.E.

In 332 B.C.E., the armies of Alexander the Great, King of Macedonia, defeated the Persian Army of Darius III and occupied the Judean Kingdom on their way to conquer Egypt.

According to legend, Jerusalem

was spared destruction thanks to a dream Alexander had many years earlier, in which he saw the High Priest of the Temple welcome him.

Following Alexander's death, rule over this part of his empire passed to his successors, the Ptolemies of Egypt and the Seleucids of Syria.

Hasmonean Period
152-37 B.C.E.

Conflicts arose between the Judeans and their Seleucid rulers. Angered by the Seleucids' desecration of their holy Temple, the Jews, under the leadership of the Hasmoneans, also known as the Maccabees, waged war against their oppressors.

Though the fighting lasted nearly 30 years, the Hasmoneans successfully defeated the Seleucids and rededicated the Temple to the service of God. Each year, Jews celebrate this victory by lighting candles on the Festival of Hanukkah.

Herod the Great
37-4 B.C.E.

Jewish kings from the Hasmonean family ruled Judea until the beginning of Roman domination, which saw a new man rise to power.

Herod, a Jew, was appointed by the Romans to the position of King. It is questionable if he was loyal to the Romans or to the Jews or only to himself. What is certain is that he was clever and effective.

Herod increased his power through marriage with Mariamne, the last heir to the Hasmonean throne, while still maintaining close relations with the

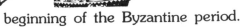

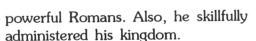

powerful Romans. Also, he skillfully administered his kingdom.

Herod launched a major building campaign in Jerusalem. Many of the remains of ancient buildings visible today were built by him, including the Western Wall and parts of the Citadel.

Roman Period
70 C.E.-324 C.E.

Following Herod's death, there were several revolts by the Jewish population. The suffering caused by high taxes as well as the disrespect that the Roman authorities showed for the Jewish religion led to a collapse of order and caused open rebellion.

In 70 C.E., after a long, bloody war, the Romans destroyed Jerusalem and burned the Temple, banning Jews from the city.

The Romans, throughout their reign, did not allow Jews to return to Jerusalem. Instead, they stationed troops in Jerusalem and rebuilt the city as Aelia Capitolina, a pagan Roman City.

A Jewish revolt, led by Shimon Bar-Kochba, in 132 C.E., enabled Jewish forces to capture Jerusalem. However, the victory was soon crushed and the Jews were once again exiled from the city.

Byzantine Period
324-638 C.E.

The Roman Emperor Constantine, a convert to Christianity, made it the official religion of the Roman Empire, marking the beginning of the Byzantine period.

Because Jerusalem is the site of many Christian holy places, interest in the city grew during this period and many churches and public buildings were constructed.

Early Islamic Period
638-1099 C.E.

Jerusalem was also holy to the Moslem prophet, Muhammad, who exerted great influence over his followers. In 638 C.E., the Moslems conquered Jerusalem, bringing an end to the Byzantine period. The Moslems built their place of prayer on the Temple Mount during this time.

Crusader Period
1099-1260 C.E.

Throughout this time, Christians in Europe continued to consider Jerusalem their holy city. They never gave up hope of returning the city to Christian control for religious as well as political and economic reasons.

In 1099, the Crusaders, European Christians, penetrated the city's defenses and conquered it from the Moslems.

Late Islamic Period
1260-1516 C.E.

After many battles with the Crusaders, the Moslems regained control over Jerusalem under the leadership of Salah ad-Din (Saladin), the Sultan of Egypt.

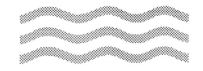

Ottoman Period
1516-1917

The Ottoman Turks, another group of Moslems, took control of Jerusalem in 1516. Many impressive sites in the city, such as the walls around the Old City of Jerusalem, were re-constructed by the Ottomans under their ruler, Suleiman the Magnificent.

During the Ottoman period, large numbers of Jews from Spain and Portugal began to settle in Jerusalem with the encouragement of the ruling Turks. Eventually, the Jews became the majority of the city's population.

British Rule
1917-1948

The British defeated the Ottoman Empire in World War I and were given control over what was then called Palestine in a mandate approved by the League of Nations.

As it became clear that the British were unable to control the growing conflict between Jews and Arabs in the land, the United Nations decided in 1947 to partition Palestine into two states, one Jewish and one Arab.

Israeli Rule
1948-Present

Israel proclaimed its independence in 1948 with Jerusalem as its capital. The Arabs attacked the fledgling Jewish State with all their might and the War of Independence began.

Half of Jerusalem was occupied by Jordan during the 1948 war. It wasn't until the Six-Day War in 1967 that Israel was able to defeat the Jordanian Army and reunite Jerusalem under Israeli rule. Since then, the city has grown to become the largest in Israel.

JERUSALEM TIME LINE:

BABYLONIAN CONQUEST
586 B.C.E.

BYZANTINE PERIOD
324-638 C.E.

KING DAVID
1004-970 B.C.E.

ROMAN PERIOD
70 C.E.-324 C.E.

JEBUSITE PERIOD
1300-1004 B.C.E.

ALEXANDER THE GREAT
332 B.C.E.